Exeter

OTHER GOODNIGHT BOOKS

Jack and the Beanstalk
The Three Little Pigs
The Tortoise and the Hare

Library of Congress Cataloging in Publication Data Andersen, Hans Christian, 1805-1875. The ugly duckling. (A Goodnight book) Translation of *Le vilain petit canard,* which was a translation of *Den grimme ælling.* SUMMARY: The new duckling is scorned by everyone because he is different, but after a lonely winter he discovers he has grown into a beautiful swan. [1. Fairy tales] I. Title. PZ8.A542Ug 1979 [E] 78-12523 ISBN 0-394-84103-4

The Ugly Duckling

ADAPTED FROM ANDERSEN
Illustrations by Lilian Obligado
Translated from the French by Ann Sperber

Alfred A. Knopf   New York

This is a Borzoi Book published by Alfred A. Knopf, Inc.

A mother duck was hatching her eggs. There were six. She could hardly wait for her babies to come out of their shells.

One day she heard a *peck, peck, peck.* The first egg cracked open. A little duckling stood in its place. *Peck, peck, peck.* A second duckling broke its shell. Then a third, and a fourth, and a fifth. The mother duck was delighted.

She turned to the sixth egg. Nothing. "Maybe it needs more hatching," she thought. She sat and waited—one day, two days, three days. On the fourth day *peck, peck, peck* the egg cracked open. The sixth little duckling had finally left its shell.

The mother duck nearly fell over when she saw him. "How ugly he is," she thought, "and how clumsy. And what a dreadful gray color! Not at all like the other children!"

She marched them to the water. All ducklings must learn to swim. The sixth duckling swam as well as his brothers and sisters but everyone on shore laughed at him—"Do

you see that awful little duckling? How ugly he is! And how clumsy!"

The mother duck turned around angrily. The ugly duckling pretended not to hear. But later he hid in the reeds and cried.

The six little ducklings grew from day to day. Their mother taught them how to waddle, how to say *quack-quack* and all the things a duck should know.

The ugly duckling was very smart and very kind and very good. But no one liked him. The other animals pulled his feathers and pecked at him and called him names. The little duckling was very unhappy. At last one day, he flew out of the barnyard. Sadly the mother duck watched him go.

He flew all day. But by nighttime he was too tired to go on. He saw a flock of wild ducks. "May I stay with you?" he asked. "Why not?" they said. "You're an ugly fellow, but if you want to stay with us, we won't trouble you."

For a few days the little duckling lived peacefully on the lake. One day *bang! bang! bang!* hunters came. Shots rang out. Two wild ducks fell dead. The ugly duckling swam into a clump of reeds and hid there, terrified.

13

That night the hunters left. The duckling crept out of his hiding place. He spread his wings and flew and flew, until he landed near a little hut. An old woman lived there with her cat and her hen.

"Good day," he said politely. "May I stay here?"

"Can you arch your back and purr?" asked the cat.

"Can you lay eggs and say *cluck-cluck?*" asked the hen.

"No," said the duckling. "But I can swim and dive and say *quack-quack.*"

"Then we don't want you here," said the old woman. She grabbed her broomstick. "Go on, get out!"

The duckling fled. He looked for a place to be alone.

Winter came. There was almost

nothing to eat. The little duckling was cold and hungry.

At last, spring came. The duckling had grown. His wings were stronger. He decided to leave the

pond and fly far away, to a new place.

He flew to a garden full of

flowers and landed on a clear and peaceful lake. Three white birds floated on the lake, the most beautiful birds he had ever seen. They were swans and they swam right toward him.

"They probably just want to peck at me and make fun of me, like everyone else," he thought.

Sadly he bowed his head. As he did, he saw his reflection in the water.

There, gazing back at him, was a magnificent white swan! The ugly duckling had not been a duck at all. He was a swan!

He had found his family at last. And together with the other swans, he lived out his days on the clear and peaceful lake, in the lovely garden.